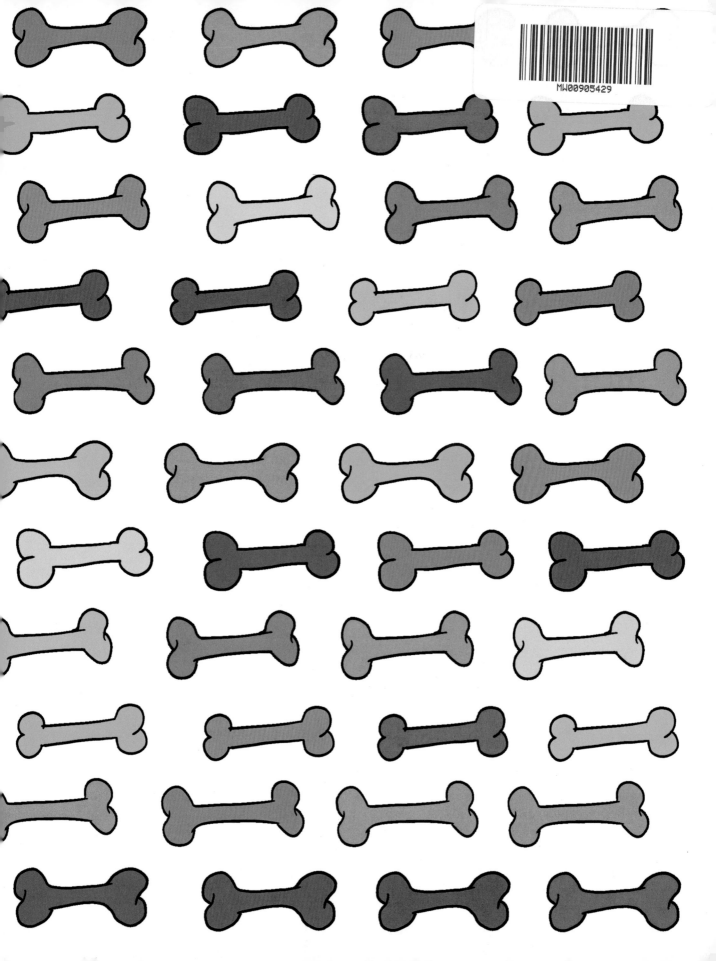

Printed in the United States of America

ISBN 978-1539789567
ISBN 153978956X

# YorkieTown

Boychick & Bear

illustrated by David M. Arnold and Matthew Trupia

In Yorkietown lived a Yorkie named Zaggy.
He was really quite sad and his tail wasn't waggy.
The problem of course is that Yorkies are small,
But Zaggy, you see, was enormously tall!

Oh how he wished and pleaded for a change,
"In a town full of talls, I wouldn't be strange."

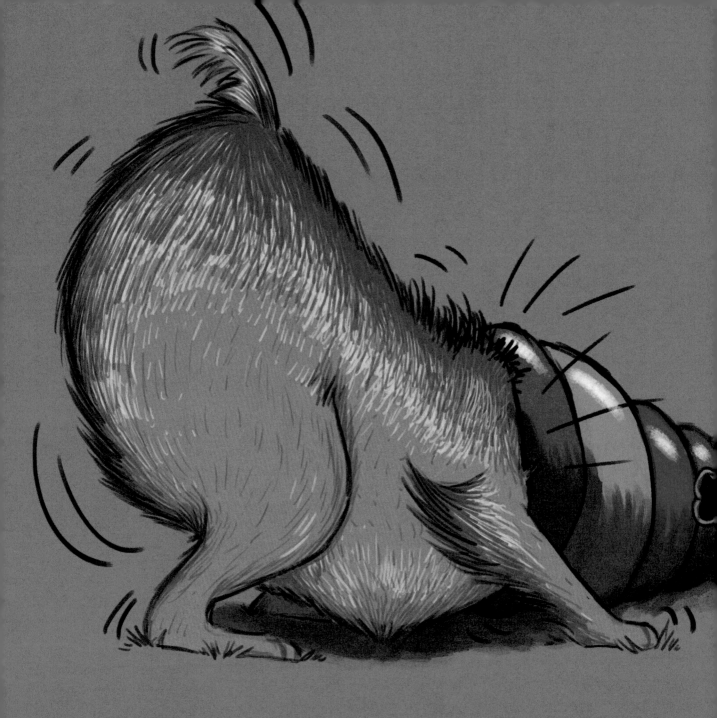

His belly was full and just a little too wide,
He couldn't scoot through the chute
No matter how hard he tried.

Zaggy had paws that were just way too big,
And a snout even larger than a barn full of pigs!

On the playground were swings
And plum colored rings,
And zip lines that swung
From aquamarine strings!

But Zaggy couldn't play
On those small Yorkie things,
For fear they could break
With a clamor of bings!

Alone all alone, he was a puppy so sad,
A sad sulky pup, no friends to be had.
So what did he do every hour all day?
He perused through his PawPad at the Yorkie Café.

He wished and he pleaded, "I need to be changed!
In a town full of talls, I wouldn't be strange."

LOOK UP TO THE SKY!

But wait, just stop, there was something awry,
His screen screeched out, "Look up to the sky!"
He looked and he leered and then it appeared,
A DUCK at the wheel of a truck with ten gears!

8

"WOOHOO! Yip yip! Gam gam! BAM BAM!
It's me, it's true, The Duckle Duck Man."

"Zaggy, I know, you're sad with your size,
Don't worry, you'll see, I have a surprise!"

Duckle Duck chuckled and professed to the pup,
"I have what you need to fix you right up!
I can fix your large size in a quickety snap,
Just a tug of this lever you'll be small just like that!

And so Zaggy's ears jerked with a perk,
He prodded the Duck, "How will this work?"

"This lever I have is so clever indeed,
It will make you quite small
In a snapety speed!"

Not a moment of fear or fright from the pup,
Zaggy lurched for the lever
And cranked it way up!

With the lever way up, way up to the sky,
Zaggy shrunk down in size
And let out a great, "Sigh!"

TUG ME

"Oh yes, oh my, I'm finally small,
I can triggle and traggle with a mini-sized ball!
I can wiggle and waggle through loopty loop rides,
I can swiggle and swaggle down the littlest slides."

Now that the pup has been fixed by the Duck,
The Duck waved goodbye and went off in his truck.

All the rest of the day,
Zaggy trotted with glee,
He played in the shade
Under cherry blossom trees.
He could scoot through the chute
With the easiest of ease,
He swung forth and back on the mini trapeze.

Right then, just now, there was something close by,
A mysterious mystery was lurking nearby.

And so it appeared at the peak of the hill,
A Doberman hound from Doberhood Ville.

This Doberhood hound had a menacing grin,
And a body with spots and orangey skin.

His ears stood straight tall, straight like a pin,
This hound had a lengthy elongated chin.

17

As the hound roamed the town,
A Yorkie pup yelped,
"We need to be saved, we need to be helped!
Get Zaggy, where's Zaggy,
He's the tallest of smalls,
He can frighten that hound
Back over those walls!"

With the largest of yipps,
Zaggy sounded his bark,
He sprinted quite quick to the Yorkietown park.
With the largest of yapps,
Zaggy made it quite clear,
"That hound will be gone,
That hound won't be near!"

19

As the Yorkietown pups
Huddled in fright,
They all seemed to notice,
"There's something not right!"

Zaggy was small,
Not the tallest of smalls,
He couldn't frighten that hound,
He couldn't at all!

The hound didn't budge,
Not a **step**, **inch** or **stride**,
He just stood
Straight and still
With the snidest
Of snides.

He cackley cackled, "You don't shake me with fear."
He wildly wackled, "You're the size of an ear!"

Zaggy exclaimed, "What should I do?"
The Yorkie pups claimed, "We wish you were you!"

That's when the skies roared a great rumble,
And Duckle Duck appeared through a funnely tunnel!

"Duckle Duck please, I need a quick change,
In this town full of smalls, I feel like I'm strange!"

As the Duck listened up at the top of his truck,
"Zaggy," he said, "You're a pup who's in luck!"

"This lever I have can reverse you quite nicely,"
So Zaggy sprung forth and gripped it quite tightly.

27

A blasty boom bupp, sounded off from the truck,
And he grew back to size of a tall Yorkie pup!

29

"Yippie, I'm me, I'm the tallest in town."
His mission was clear,

"Get rid of that hound!"

He woofed and he barked
With a loud swilly shrill,
"Be gone, go away to your Doberhood Ville!"

The hound shook in his fur

And he shivered in fright

And he cowered down low

At Zaggy's towering height!

With a hurriedly scurry, the hound sniffled away,
And the Yorkie pups cheered, "Zaggy saved us today!"

On this day it was clear,
Zaggy's proud of his size,
"I see that my size is truly a prize.
I love being tall, not small like them all,
The tallest of smalls is who I am after all!"

33

Manufactured by Amazon.com
Columbia, SC
01 April 2017